VISA
OPEN
OPEN
MONDAY 10 - 5
TUESDAY 10 - 5
WEDNESDAY 2 - 8
THURSDAY 10 - 5
FRIDAY 10 - 8
SATURDAY 2 - 5
VISA

Snips
hair salon
SUPER
conditioner
for hair
Shampoo
HAIR
RESTORER
Hair
grease

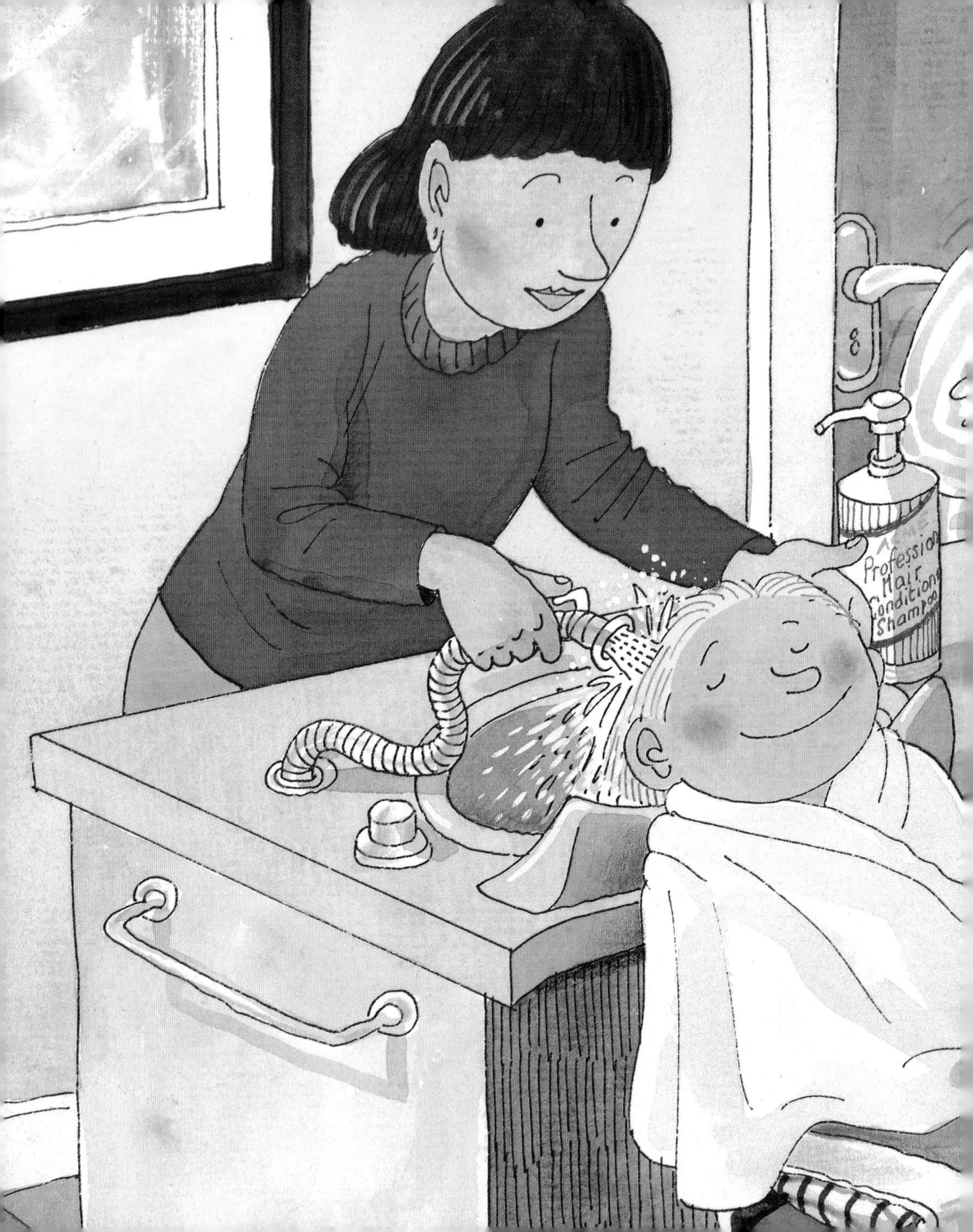
ACME
Professio
Hair
Condition
Shampoo

Hair Gel
Hair

Hair Spray
Spray